THE ADVENTURES OF
Laura Rose & Ashley Marie

A Lovely Bubbly Day

Dedication

I dedicate this first book to my mother,

Myrnetta Read (Holden).

Acknowledgements

I thank the publisher Susan Smyth, the
editors Jane Hunter and Pamela Lucier, as well as
the illustrator Liizah Radforth, who have turned my
dream into a reality.

 AT-HOME Publications

Published By  AT-HOME Publications

R.R #1, Rockwood, Ontario N0B 2K0

For a complete list of titles in print visit our
website at: www.at-homepublications.com

Canadian Cataloguing in Publication Data

van de Wiel, Debi, 1952-
    A Lovely Bubbly Day

(The Adventures of Laura Rose and Ashley Marie; 1)
ISBN 1-894125-16-9

    I. Radforth, Liizah II. Title III. Series: van de Wiel, Debi,
1952-
Adventures of Laura Rose and Ashley Marie; 1.

PS8593.A53875L68 1999   jC813'.54   C99-900033-0
PZ7.V28523Lo 1999

Editors: Jane Hunter and Pamela Lucier
Copy Editor: Matthew Bunch
Layout and Design: Pamela Lucier
Cover Design and Graphics: Catherine Bould
Film: David Briggs

Printed in Canada

A Lovely Bubbly Day

CONTENTS

Acknowledgements

Chapter 1

Laura Rose of Nova Scotia 4

Chapter 2

Ashley Marie and the Stamp Business 19

Chapter 3

Plans and Dreams 30

Chapter 4

Bubbles and Giggles 42

Chapter 5

The Mess 50

Chapter 6

The Rescue 59

Illustrated by Liizah Radforth

Chapter One
Laura Rose of Nova Scotia

Laura Rose King sat cross-legged on the kitchen floor patting her dalmatian, Thoreau. Her dad had given Thoreau to her last Christmas to keep her company. Laura Rose was an only child and her dad, Harrison King, was a single parent who loved and nurtured his daughter.

Laura Rose had lots of family and friends in the rural community of Maccan, Nova Scotia, a ten minute drive from Amherst. Her best friend was her cousin, Ashley Marie Burbidge. They were both eight years old and had a special bond. Both Laura Rose and Ashley Marie were adopted by different

members of the same family when they were babies.

Laura Rose's thick, blue-black hair, which was cut like a bowl, framed her oval face. Her round blue eyes shone like sapphires, just like her Grampie's. Harrison, Laura Rose's Dad, sometimes teased her and called her "raven." Ashley Marie, on the other hand, had blonde, wavy hair that fell below her shoulders, with one little curl that hung down in the middle of her forehead. She also had three little dimples on her heart-shaped face. Her almond-shaped brown eyes gave all her secrets away.

Le Chat, the cat, slinked over to Laura Rose and Thoreau on the floor. Le Chat walked back and forth in front of Thoreau, swaying its racoon-coloured tail. Thoreau paid no attention. Le Chat then stole over to Laura Rose and sat in front of her. Le Chat stared at Laura Rose through large green eyes.

"Scat, Le Chat," said Laura Rose as she gently pushed Le Chat away. "Don't tease Thoreau." Le Chat slanted her eyes, her ears stood up, and her tail waved back and forth furiously.

"I think her food dish is empty, Laura Rose," said Mrs. Whang who was busy cleaning the kitchen stove.

Laura Rose got up and went to the cupboard for the cat food. She spooned a little of it into Le Chat's dish. "Now I hope you're happy," said Laura Rose.

Laura Rose sat down at the kitchen table. She put her elbows on the table, cupping her little face in her hands. "Is everything okay?" asked Mrs. Whang.

"It's hot today," Laura Rose replied quietly.

Ever since Laura Rose's mother had died two years ago of breast cancer, Mrs. Whang felt like a mother to the little girl. Mr. King hired Mrs. Whang to clean house, make meals, and look after Laura Rose during the summer months. Mrs. Whang is married. Her husband is a pharmacist and her daughter is studying at university so that she can follow in her father's footsteps.

Mrs. Whang continued cleaning. She wanted everything to be squeaky clean. She thought about Laura Rose and her father, Harrison King. Mrs. Whang loved the little girl and had a great deal of respect for her father. She knew Mr. King missed his wife, Laurel Ivy, and she also knew that he loved his daughter, Laura Rose, dearly.

Laura Rose interrupted Mrs. Whang's thoughts.

"Mrs. Whang, do you think Dad will marry Shayla?"

"I don't know, honey," said Mrs. Whang. "Would you like that?"

"Dad doesn't need anybody else but me, and we have you to look after us," said Laura Rose.

Mrs. Whang listened and continued shining the stove.

"If they marry," continued Laura Rose, "she'll be my stepmother and fairytales say stepmothers are wicked, so I don't want them to get married."

Mrs. Whang looked seriously at Laura Rose. "Wicked stepmothers are only in fairy-tales, sweetie," said Mrs. Whang, "and fairy-tales aren't true. Shayla is a kind person and she loves you and your ..."

Just then the phone rang, interrupting their conversation. Laura Rose jumped from the chair and ran down the hall to pick it up.

"Hiya Ashley," answered Laura Rose. She listened thoughtfully to Ashley.

"Do you want to trade stamps and wash some Barbie clothes? We could even go with Grampie to cut Alders."

"Maybe," commented Laura Rose. I'll go ask Dad and be right back."

Laura Rose placed the phone on the round hall table and ran down the basement stairs.

Mrs. Whang continued cleaning and thought about Laura Rose and her father. She was very happy working for Mr. King and she loved Laura Rose like her own daughter. It was so sad that her mother had died of cancer. "Such a terrible disease," thought Mrs. Whang, "and Laurel Ivy King was so young and always so happy."

Mrs. Whang was glad Laura Rose's father had a woman friend. Mrs. Whang remembered the day Mr. King and Shayla met. One of Mr. King's friends arranged a blind date for him with Shayla. They enjoyed the day sailing around Pugwash, Nova Scotia. They became friends. Mrs. Whang thought it would be good for Mr. King and Shayla to get married someday, then Laura Rose would have a mother again. Even though Laura Rose had her father it wasn't the same thing. Besides, Harrison King was a writer who, like many writers, buried himself in his work. This summer he was writing a book for children about dinosaur fossils found in Parrsboro, Nova Scotia.

Harrison King's friend, Shayla Martines, had immigrated from the Dominican Republic to Nova Scotia and taught computer classes at the high school. Shayla's family still lives in the Dominican Republic. But Shayla had dreamed of coming to Canada ever since she met Canadian tourists at the resort where she used to work in her homeland.

Mrs. Whang stopped cleaning and decided it was time to make iced tea. Mr. King would be ready for a break. He had been in the basement all morning working on his book.

"Dad, Dad," said Laura Rose. "Ashley wants me to go to her place. Can I go? Please, Dad, please!"

Harrison King looked up from his computer and pile of papers. "Come here, raven," said Mr. King, "and we'll have a little chat about this."

Laura Rose climbed into her Dad's lap and he gave her a hug. "Can I bike to Ashley's and stay the afternoon?" asked Laura Rose.

"Well, let's see raven. What are you going to do?" asked Harrison.

"Maybe trade stamps, wash some Barbie clothes, and go with Grampie to cut Alders, Dad," answered Laura Rose.

"Your Grampie is always doing something," said Harrison. Thomas Zebulah Burbidge, Harrison's deceased wife's father, was now 70 years old. His health was good except for a bad back which slowed him down a bit. He kept himself busy on the farm and helped tend blueberry fields - or so he told everyone. Most of the time Thomas went fishing or busied himself making beautiful things out of wood for his grandchildren. Thank goodness his son James and grandson, Zeb, helped run the farm. Zeb was ten and he was a big help with the animals.

Laura Rose patted her Dad's leg. "Can I

go, Dad, on my bike, please?"

"Yes you can, raven," said her father, "on three conditions: don't talk to any strangers on the road, call me as soon as you get to Ashley's, and be ready when I pick you up at 6:00 o'clock. Shayla is going to cook us a special dinner tonight."

He set Laura Rose on the floor, hugged and kissed her, then turned back to the computer.

"Thanks Dad," said Laura Rose, "I'll remember the three conditions."

"Bye Laura Rose," said her father.

"Bye," replied Laura Rose. Laura Rose ran back upstairs.

"Ashley ... Ash..."

There was no answer on the other end of

the phone. "Are you still there Ashley?" asked Laura Rose.

"I thought you forgot all about me," said Ashley.

"I'm biking to your place right now," said Laura Rose.

"Don't forget your Bugs Bunny stamp and I got a Winnie the Pooh stamp for you," said Ashley.

"I told you Ashley, I want two stamps for my Bugs Bunny. My stamp came all the way from the United States, so it's worth more," said Laura Rose. "Ashley just didn't know the value of a Bugs Bunny stamp," thought Laura Rose.

"They are worth the same to me because I love Winnie the Pooh and Bugs Bunny," replied Ashley.

"My stamp costs more money," insisted
Laura Rose.

"Well Laura Rose, I read in the newspa-
per that a Winnie the Pooh stamp sold for
$9.95," stated Ashley.

"When did you start reading newspapers,
Ashley?" asked Laura Rose.

"Since Grammie said it was a good habit
to get into," answered Ashley. "Anyway I've
got to help Mum with Joshua Lee. We can talk
more when you get here."

"I'm leaving now. Bye," said Laura Rose.

"See ya soon," replied Ashley. The phone
went dead. Laura Rose ran upstairs and got
her Bugs Bunny stamp and put it in the back
pocket of her jeans. "I won't take any Barbie

clothes with me," thought Laura Rose. "This stamp deal will take all afternoon."

"Bye Mrs. Whang," said Laura Rose. "I'm biking to Ashley's. Bye Thoreau. Bye Le Chat."

"Bye Laura Rose. Have fun. Don't forget to wear your bike helmet," said Mrs. Whang, "and call us when you get to Ashley's."

Chapter Two
Ashley Marie and The Stamp Business

Laura Rose grabbed her helmet off the porch floor and put it on as she ran out the door. She jumped on her blue bike and pedalled along the dirt road to Ashley's house. The girls did not live too far apart so Laura Rose decided to take her time and think about this stamp business. Her mother had loved to collect stamps since she was a little girl and she used to trade with her friends. She gave her collection to Laura Rose, which her father called a family tradition. Laura Rose talked Ashley Marie into starting her own. They both loved to look at the miniature pictures on the stamps. Trading was fun, but she heard

her Grampie say that business with family members doesn't always work out well.

Laura Rose stopped at the bridge crossing over the river. She always stopped to look for frogs and lizards sunning on the river bank or to watch minnows move quickly near the surface of the water. She spied a speckled trout in a deep pool in the river. Her dad told her there used to be plenty of trout when he was a little boy.

Laura Rose looked down at her Mickey Mouse watch. It was 1:00 o'clock. "I better get going," thought Laura Rose, "or Dad will be worried." She hopped on her bike again. A movement behind her caught her attention. She saw Ashley's older brother, Zeb biking fast. It looked like he was trying to catch

Laura Rose. She pedalled as fast as she could. Zeb was two years older, so he thought that he was smarter and stronger than Laura Rose and his sister, Ashley.

"I'm gonna race you to the house, Laura Rose," Zeb called out.

Laura Rose pedalled a little faster. "Dad always said to be careful biking on the dirt road," thought Laura Rose. "But I don't want Zeb to win."

Once at the bottom of the hill, Laura Rose pedalled around the bend and over the culvert. There was the driveway to Ashley's house. At the foot of the driveway by the mailbox, she jumped off her bike and waited for Zeb.

Zeb rode past her as if she wasn't even standing there. "Hi Zeb. Hot day," said Laura Rose.

Zeb turned back to Laura Rose and shouted, "You had a head start or I would have won."

"Thank you, Zebulah Thomas, Jr.," Laura Rose replied. Laura Rose called Zeb by his full name because she knew that he didn't like it and she wanted to annoy him.

Laura Rose jumped on her bike and pedalled up the driveway. She could see Zeb heading for his treehouse, probably to pout.

Laura Rose pedalled up the hill to the old farmhouse where Ashley lived. Laura Rose loved that old grey shingled house. It had been in the family for over 100 years. The house was long and had four gable windows upstairs in the front. You could see the Bay of Fundy from every room and some evenings, you could even see the lights in New Brunswick. A verandah ran the length of the house. On the verandah there was a white porch swing and plenty of wicker furniture with cushions made by her Grammie. Rose bushes grew along the entire length of the verandah. Ashley was sitting on the swing on the old verandah.

It was a hot day, but once in a while there was a rose-scented breeze. Her Mum and Grammie had all kinds of flowers, but they especially liked the old country rose bushes that were planted around the verandah.

Ashley was holding her nine-month old brother, Joshua Lee, and was singing him to sleep. "Tell me why the stars do shine, tell me why the ivy twines, then tell me why the sky is blue, and I will tell you, why I love you....cause hummmmmmmm, the stars shine, hummmmmmm." Ashley couldn't remember all the words to the song, but Joshua Lee had finally closed his eyes. Ashley continued to swing and hum the tune softly. She heard Grammie sing this song many times while she played the piano. It was Grampie's favorite song.

Ashley looked down at her stamp collection laying on the verandah floor. She wanted that Bugs Bunny stamp, but Laura Rose could be stubborn and hard to deal with sometimes.

"I'll give her one Winnie the Pooh and that old Queen Victoria stamp that came with the collection. That's all she's getting," Ashley muttered to Joshua Lee.

Laura Rose spied Ashley on the verandah with the baby, Joshua Lee. "Hey Ash," shouted Laura Rose. She leaned her bike against the verandah step. Ashley placed her finger over her lips. "Sh!"

Laura Rose stepped quietly onto the verandah. "I just have to call Dad so he knows I'm here, Ashley," whispered Laura Rose. Laura Rose opened the screen door quietly and went in the house. After calling home, she returned to the verandah where Ashley was still humming to Joshua Lee.

"Can I see the Winnie the Pooh stamp?" whispered Laura Rose as she bent down and kissed Joshua Lee's forehead. He smelled of baby powder.

Ashley pointed to her stamp book. Laura Rose bent over and picked the stamp book up off the floor.

"Please don't pick up my stamps with your fingers, Laura Rose," whispered Ashley. "You have to use the tweezers over there on the table."

Laura Rose turned the pages of Ashley's book until she found the Winnie the Pooh stamp.

"What stamp do you want for your Bugs Bunny?" whispered Ashley.

"I would like two Winnie the Pooh stamps for my Bugs Bunny," answered Laura Rose quietly.

"Two Winnie the Pooh for one Bugs Bunny!" exclaimed Ashley a little bit loudly.

Joshua Lee's eyes opened and he fussed a bit. Laura Rose placed her finger over her lips, "Sh!"

"I'll give you one Winne the Pooh and this beautiful Queen of England from 1901," whispered Ashley.

"Who's the Queen?" asked Laura Rose.

"Queen Victoria. She made Christmas what it is today. There is also a holiday every May in her honor. That's a very important stamp, Laura Rose," replied Ashley.

"I don't know," Laura Rose replied, still

not quite convinced. "You can't buy Bugs in Canada," she continued. "But, if the Queen is that important, I guess I'll trade my Bugs Bunny stamp for one Winnie the Pooh and the Queen stamp." Laura Rose took her Bugs Bunny out of her jeans pocket and placed it in Ashley's stamp book with the tweezers. She then removed her Winnie the Pooh and Queen Victoria stamps and put them in her back pocket. When the stamp business was over, Laura Rose sat on the swing beside Ashley and the baby.

Chapter Three
Plans and Dreams

"Who's all inside with your Mum?" whispered Laura Rose. The girls could hear women's voices through the old wooden screen door. They were laughing and talking and they could hear their Aunt Bunnie squeal with delight.

"Joy, this is an absolutely beautiful piece of material," said Aunt Bunnie. "Wasn't this one of Ashley's first skating outfits? And this is Zeb's first baseball uniform."

"Yes," answered Ashley's mother, Joy. "Every piece we are sewing in this quilt is clothing from each member of this family."

"Have you named the quilt yet, Joy?" asked Aunt Bunnie.

"Yes, the Heirloom Quilt," answered Joy. "I hope we get it finished in time for the 4H competition in September."

"We will," stated Grammie, "if we stop talking." The room went quiet.

Joshua Lee started to cry. He looked up at Ashley and put his little fists in his mouth. "Here's your soother, JL," whispered Ashley. "Don't cry because Mummy's busy."

Ashley preferred to call her little brother "JL." Joshua Lee seemed like such a big name for a little guy, but Grampie was always saying "that Joshua Lee is built like a football player."

Just then Ashley's Mom walked through the door. "Lunch time Joshua Lee," Ashley's Mom said as she picked up the little boy.

"Hello Laura Rose. I didn't know you were here honey. You young ladies are so quiet."

Laura Rose loved her Aunt Joy. It was like having a Mom around. Laura Rose got up, went over, and hugged her Aunt Joy. "Ashley is lucky to have a mom," thought Laura Rose. Laura Rose missed her own mom a lot.

"Now what are you two going to do this afternoon?" asked Aunt Joy.

"We were thinking," said Ashley, "maybe we could wash our Barbie doll clothes in the kitchen sink, the one with the old pump.

Then Grampie is taking us to the brook to cut trees."

"That sounds good, but I don't want you two bothering Grampie or your father, Ashley."

"They are busy with the farm and the blueberry fields this time of year," said Ashley's mom.

James, Ashley Marie's Dad, was a hard worker and helped Grampie Thomas with everything.

The farm and blueberries have been in the Burbidge family for about one hundred years. Joy knew Grampie had high hopes that it would always stay in the family. Joy was happy that Zeb, her son, showed an interest in the farm, but she knew that he was more interested in baseball.

"Maybe one of the girls or Joshua Lee will want to farm. Plenty of time for their future," Joy thought as she smiled to herself.

"Sorry girls," said Joy, "I was lost in thought. You two run along and I'll feed Joshua Lee and put him to bed."

"Grampie promised to take us today to cut trees, Mum," answered Ashley.

"If it's not today, it'll be another day, Ashley. The Alders aren't going anywhere. So you and Laura Rose go wash your Barbie doll clothes and don't forget to clean up your mess."

The two girls raced up the stairs to Ashley's bedroom. Everything in Ashley's bedroom was green, her favorite color. There were pictures of skaters on every wall. Her bookcase was lined with books. Ashley loved her books, some of which she had read more than twice. Her skating trophies and ribbons were proudly displayed on a shelf.

"I'm going to be a hockey player, and I'm going to be in the Olympics someday, Laura Rose," Ashley announced.

"Sure," answered Laura Rose. "I thought you were going to be a figure skater in the Olympics?" Laura Rose thought , "The hockey player business is a new one today!"

"Well, I'll be one or the other. There is a girl's hockey team in the Olympics now," said Ashley.

Both girls carried an armful of doll clothes down the back stairs to the old part of the kitchen. They could hear the women talking and laughing in the dining room. "Laura Rose, let's go look at the quilt before we wash these clothes," said Ashley.

Both girls put the Barbie doll clothes on the counter and went down the hallway to the dining room. The ladies were just sitting around enjoying their tea and sweets. Their Auntie Margaret saw them first. "Ashley Marie! Laura Rose! Come in and let us see you," said Auntie Margaret.

The ladies all turned to the girls.

"Come on in," said their Grammie, Martha Coreen.

Both girls were a bit shy, although most of the women were relatives or friends of the family.

"You've both grown this summer and your faces are so tanned and fresh looking from being outdoors," commented Aunt Bunnie.

"Help yourself to some sweets, Ashley and Laura Rose," said Grammie.

"No thank you Grammie," said Ashley. "Laura Rose and I want to wash our Barbie doll clothes and get them dry this afternoon. But first we wanted to look at the quilt."

The girls peered down at the bright yellow quilt with squares of bright coloured material sewn on the top. "This is beautiful, Grammie," said Laura Rose.

"Your Aunt Joy is going to enter this quilt in the 4H competition in Truro," said Grammie.

"I hope Mum wins," replied Ashley.

"We hope so too," stated a smiling Auntie Margaret.

Auntie Margaret travelled around the world with her husband who worked for the Pearson Peacekeeping Centre near Clementsport, Nova Scotia. They had just come back home from England. Auntie Margaret reached in her purse and handed an envelope to both Ashley and Laura Rose.

The girls opened their envelopes and inside each was a stamp. "Oh, thank you, Auntie Margaret," exclaimed a very excited Laura Rose. "This is a Lady Diana stamp."

"Thank you, Auntie Margaret," said Ashley. "She is so pretty. I'm going to put this in my stamp collection book right away."

"You're both very welcome," said Auntie Margaret. "Now come and give me a big hug." Both girls hugged their Auntie Margaret.

"Well," said Grammie, "I think it's time to start quilting again or we're never going to get the quilt finished for this fall."

"We're going into the old kitchen, Grammie, to wash doll clothes," said Ashley.

"Put your stamps away first," said Grammie.

Ashley and Laura Rose went out onto the verandah and with the tweezers Ashley very carefully placed her new stamp into her collection book.

"You can put your stamps in here too, Laura Rose," said Ashley. Laura Rose carefully placed her Winnie the Pooh, Queen Victoria, and Lady Diana stamps next to Ashley's. Then the two girls went back into the house to the old kitchen.

Chapter Four
Bubbles and Giggles

Ashley pulled a chair over to the high sink, climbed up on it, and dumped all the Barbie doll clothes in the basin. "We need soap to wash the clothes," said Laura Rose as she climbed on top of the cupboard.

Ashley climbed off the chair and nosed around under the sink. "I think this is the soap Mum uses, but I don't know how much to use."

"Just pour it in the basin and I'll start pumping the handle," said Laura Rose.

Ashley poured half the bottle of soap into the water. Bubbles started very slowly. So Ashley poured more soap into the basin. The

43

bubbles started to rise higher and higher in the basin. Then the bubbles moved slowly over the counter. Bubbles floated in the air and down the sides of the cupboard. Laura Rose kept pumping the water.

The girls giggled. "This is great fun," Ashley said.

Laura Rose pumped water harder. Bubbles flew everywhere. Ashley threw handfuls of bubbles at Laura Rose. Laura Rose took two handfuls and blew bubbles on top of Ashley's head. They tossed bubbles high in the air. The girls cupped bubbles in their hands and blew them at each other. They laughed and giggled.

The bubbles kept pouring out of the sink. Ashley couldn't see her feet for bubbles!

Laura Rose couldn't stand it any longer on top of the sink and down she came to dance in the bubbles.

"I'm a perfect skater, Laura Rose," said Ashley as she skated through the bubbles. "This would be a great act while I'm skating in front of people. Bubbles everywhere."

"And the bubbles could be every colour of the rainbow," said Laura Rose.

"We better finish these clothes, then we can come back and play in the bubbles some more," said Ashley.

The girls climbed back on the chairs and rooted through the bubbles for their doll clothes. They kept throwing bubbles and laughing. They found the clothes and rung them out.

They took the clothes outdoors to hang them on the clothesline, but Ashley's Mom had filled the clothesline. She hung clothes out every day to dry.

Ashley looked at Laura Rose. She mimicked her mother: "Oh Ashley, I surely love the smell of the outdoors on our clothes." The girls giggled.

"Now where are we going to dry them?" asked a serious Laura Rose.

"Let's take them to the barn. There are a lot of places to hang them or lay them flat," said Ashley.

They carried the clothes to the barn and went in.

"Meow Meow Meow," greeted Jasmine, Ashley's cat.

"Hi Jasmine," the girls said together.

They looked around to find a spot to hang their clothes. Jasmine followed them. She had just given birth to four kittens and she was making sure nobody found them.

"Did you find Jasmine's kittens?" asked Laura Rose.

"No and she won't take us to them," said Ashley. "Grampie and I tried to find them the other day, but Jasmine hides her kittens well. She's a good mother."

Swallows swooped low as they flew in and out of the barn. Their mud and straw nests were built high on the barn rafters. As they flew, their mouths caught the flying insects.

Carrying their bundle of clothes, the girls walked past the empty pig stalls.

"We could lay the clothes over the pig stalls," suggested Laura Rose.

"No. Pigs eat everything including clothes," replied Ashley.

"The pigs are all outside and the clothes will be dry by the time they return to the barn," argued Laura Rose.

Jasmine rubbed herself against Ashley's leg.

"Okay," agreed Ashley, "and then we'll go back to the house and clean up the kitchen like Mum asked."

The girls gently laid each piece of clothing over the walls of the pig stall. The girls left happily. Laura Rose whistled all the way back to the house. Ashley tried to whistle, but only air escaped her lips.

"I can't whistle, Laura Rose," stated Ashley.

"Sure you can. Everyone can whistle," replied Laura Rose. "Just push your lips out like you do when you give JL a kiss, then blow a note. Just watch me."

Ashley watched Laura Rose. She tried again and again to whistle. Only air came out. She shrugged her shoulders and listened to Laura Rose whistle away.

Chapter Five
The Mess

The girls reached the house, went through the back porch and into the room filled with bubbles, which were up to their knees. There stood Grammie with a very unhappy look on her face.

"Ashley Marie! Laura Rose! What is going on here? Where did all these bubbles come from?"

The girls giggled.

"Grammie..."

"Ashley Marie, this is not a giggling matter. You get these bubbles cleaned up right now before your mother gets in here!" said the girls' Grammie. "She has company and

enough work all day without having to clean this up."

Ashley thought about scooping up bubbles in both hands and blowing them at her Grammie, but that wouldn't be nice. Instead, she blew some in Laura Rose's face. Their Grammie then kicked bubbles across the floor and both girls kicked bubbles back. Soon they were all laughing.

"Now now, young ladies. Let's clean this up before your mother comes, Ashley Marie," said Grammie.

Grammie left the room and returned with two mops and two buckets. She gave one mop and bucket to Ashley and Laura Rose. Grammie took the other and helped the girls.

"We should just let the bubbles disappear

on their own," said Laura Rose.

"Bubbles don't just disappear, Laura Rose. Haven't you ever watched what happens to bubbles?" Ashley asked.

"Not lately. I'm too busy with stamps," answered Laura Rose. The girls giggled.

"I have a great idea," said Ashley. "This mop and bucket takes too long. Hold the back door open, Laura Rose."

Ashley took her bucket and scooped the bubbles up, carrying them out the door, and dumped them on the ground.

"I'll use your bucket, Grammie," said Laura Rose, "and do the same thing."

Before long there was a mountain of bubbles beside the back steps. The bubbles looked like a mountain of snow. Laura Rose and Ashley watched the bubbles. Pop, pop, pop! The biggest bubbles burst, then disappeared. The mountain of bubbles turned into small fluffy clouds, which turned into a puddle of water.

"I love listening to bubbles," said Ashley.

They went back into the kitchen and Grammie had just finished mopping up the floor.

"How much soap did you two use?" asked Grammie.

"I think we used too much," answered Ashley quietly.

"I think you used that whole bottle of soap on that little bit of clothing," said Grammie. "You only need a tiny bit of soap."

Grammie took the mops and buckets back into the back porch.

"Maybe we should go check to see if our clothes are dry," suggested Ashley. "I don't think Grammie has finished saying what's on her mind."

"Uh huh." agreed Laura Rose. "We better go out the front door and if she doesn't see us maybe she'll forget about it."

The girls tiptoed down the hallway, past the dining-room where the women were working on the quilt, and walked out the screen door onto the verandah without anyone noticing them.

"Where are you two going in such a hurry?" shouted Zeb from his treehouse.

Laura Rose and Ashley ran to the barn without answering Zeb.

They went through the narrow barn door. They heard pigs grunting, snorting, and squealing. They looked towards the pig stall. No doll clothes were to be seen.

"Where are our doll clothes?" Ashley cried out.

"I don't know," declared Laura Rose, a puzzled look on her face.

They walked over to the pig stall. Two pigs were playing tug-a-war with one of Barbie's sweaters. A baby pig had one of Barbie's dresses on its head and was running around the stall. Mamma pig was snorting and grunting, and digging her hoofs into a pile of Barbie doll clothes. The clothes were covered with filthy mud and manure. The girls stood there with their mouths open.

"Catching flies you two?" asked Zeb.

The girls turned to see Zeb, who was sitting on a pile of hay and chewing on a piece of Timothy.

"Never mind, Zeb Thomas," said Ashley Marie.

Zeb laughed.

"What's all the noise in my barn?"

The girls turned to see their Grampie. They turned back to Zeb, then to their Grampie. Their eyes turned back to the pig stall.

Zeb was laughing. "Look what those girls did, Gramp."

Grampie walked over to Ashley and Laura Rose and peered into the pig stall. They watched mama pig dig more clothes into the filthy mess in the stall.

"Are those doll clothes in with my pigs?" asked Grampie, a twinkle in his bright blue eyes. He looked down at the two quiet girls. They stood there moon-eyed at the scene inside the pig stall.

Chapter Six
The Rescue

The swallows soared around the top of the barn. Then they glided low to see what was going on in their usually quiet home.

"Our Barbie doll clothes are a mess, Grampie," stated Ashley softly.

"I can certainly see that even without my glasses," replied Grampie.

"I'll get those clothes for you," said Grampie. "Zeb, hand me the bucket over by Bessie Lou's stall."

Grampie opened the small gate leading into the pig stall.

"Get! Get!" said Grampie as he clapped his hands. The pigs scurried off into a corner of their home.

"Coo coo. Coo coo." A dove flew into the barn and over the scene to watch Grampie rescue the clothes.

Zeb went into the pig stall and both he and Grampie put the filthy doll clothes into the bucket.

"Get! Get!" stated Zeb, as the little pig nosed around. The baby pig squealed with delight.

When the clothes were all gathered up, Grampie carried the bucket out to the two girls.

What looked like Barbie's tennis outfit lay on top of the pile.

"Yuck!" exclaimed Laura Rose.

"These clothes will never come clean," wailed Ashley.

Plop! White droppings fell on the tennis outfit as the dove flew over.

"I don't think this is the place to dry clothes," said Laura Rose.

"We have to wash them all over again," said a sad Ashley.

"Now now, girls," said Grampie. "We'll take these clothes to the pump and fill the bucket with water. If we rinse them off well you can wash them again and they'll look like brand new."

Laura Rose looked down at her Mickey Mouse watch.

"I can't go to cut Alders today, Grampie,"

stated Laura Rose. "Dad is picking me up at six o'clock."

"We'll get Alders another day," answered Grampie, "when you can come with us Laura Rose."

"Can we go in the wagon you made us, Grampie?" asked Ashley.

"Yes yes," said Grampie, "but we better get these clothes rinsed out right now. Come along."

Zeb carried the bucket of clothes and they all walked over to the pump.

Zeb set the bucket under the spout. Laura Rose grabbed the handle and pumped as fast and as hard as she could.

"You're good at that Laura Rose," said Grampie as water poured quickly into the bucket.

"Laura Rose had lots of practice today, Grampie," replied Ashley.

The girls giggled.

Grampie looked at the girls, shook his head, and started to laugh. His old straw hat, which usually sat on the back of his head, fell off. Zeb started laughing too.

"One minute you're sad. The next you're giggling," said Grampie. "You must be tired."

"It's been a giggly day," said Ashley Marie.

"A lovely bubbly day!" added Laura Rose.